PUZZLES FROM THE PAST

Pooja Lulla

Illustrations
Shreya Sen

SCHOLASTIC
New York Toronto London Auckland
Sydney New Delhi Hong Kong

CONTENTS

PUZZLES

FROM THE PAST

Published by Scholastic India Pvt. Ltd.
A subsidiary of Scholastic Inc., New York, 10012 (USA).
Publishers since 1920, with international operations in Canada, Australia, New Zealand, the United Kingdom, India, and Hong Kong.

For information regarding permission, write to:
Scholastic India Pvt. Ltd.
A-27, Ground Floor, Bharti Sigma Centre
Infocity-1, Sector 34, Gurgaon-122001 (India)

First edition: August 2018

ISBN-13: 978-93-5275-559-2

Printed at MicroPrints (India), New Delhi

1. THE MILK MAN

Children love milk. Most of them like it creamy and white. Many others like to dunk cookies in milk for milk makes cookies delicious to bite. But do you know who showed the world how to make milk safe to drink? It was a scientist who lived in France in the 19th century. Cross out the letters in the even-numbered boxes. The remaining letters will give you this scientist's name.

1	2	3	4	5	6	7	8	9	10	11	12	13	14	15	16	17	18	19	20	21	22	23
L	K	O	M	U	J	I	G	S		P	R	A	N	S	D	T	W	E	Q	U	Y	R

2. THE GENIUS FROM PISA

Galileo Galilei was born in 1564 in Pisa, the town in Italy famous for the Leaning Tower. He was an astronomer, who loved gazing at stars, a scientist, a musician and a mathematician too. But Galileo is most famous for improving the useful invention you can see him looking through in the picture. It lets you see things that are far away. Find out what this invention is called by writing the first two letters of the picture clues given below.

_ _lesco_ _

3. THE EXPLORER'S SHIPS

In 1492, Christopher Columbus set sail for the Indies but landed up in North America. Here he met the Native Indians, whom he called Indians because he was convinced that he had landed in India. Many of this 15th century Italian explorer's voyages were gifts from the king and queen of Spain and completed in his three famous ships. You can see these ships in the picture. But oops, the letters that form their names have been scrambled up. Put the letters in the correct order to find the names of Columbus' ships.

4. WORLD'S FAVOURITE STORYTELLERS

Once upon a time in Germany, there lived two brothers—Jacob and Wilhelm. They wrote some of the world's most famous stories. There is a famous one about a girl who met a wolf on the way to her grandmother's house. Another story is about a girl who had very long hair and lived in a tower. Most people know the brothers by their last name. Write the first letters of the picture clues in the blank spaces to find out what the brothers' last name is.

___ ___ ___ ___ ___

5. FIRST MEN ON THE MOON

They were the first men to walk on the moon. They were there for almost 21 hours. They brought moon rocks to Earth for everyone to see, and made their country, the United States of America, and the whole world very proud. Solve the first clue to find the name of the man who walked on the moon first. Then fill the blank spaces with the sound the insect on the TV makes to know the name of the man who followed him.

_ _ _ _ ALDRIN

6. THE LITTLE MUSICIAN

Mozart was born in the middle of the 18th century in Salzburg, now in Austria. He began playing the keyboard at the age of three. When he was just six, he played the piano at the Imperial Palace in Vienna, with the keyboard covered! Mozart went on to write six hundred pieces of music and become one of the world's most famous musicians. Mozart's first name is hidden in the grid. Follow the instructions and find out what it is.

INSTRUCTIONS

Cross out all the Zs, Vs, Bs and Js. Fill in the blanks with the remaining letters to get Mozart's first name.

_ _ _ _ _ _ _ _

W	J	Z	B	G	J	Z	V
B	O	V	F	Z	A	V	G
V	B	J	Z	J	B	J	B
Z	B	L	J	B	Z	N	Z

7. A LOVING HUSBAND

The Taj Mahal, in India, is counted among the Seven Wonders of the World. It was built in the 17th century by a famous Mughal emperor who wanted a beautiful resting place for his dead wife. And so he spent 22 long years building this magnificent marble monument. Break the code to find out this emperor's name.

_ _ _ _ _ _ _ _ _

RGZG IZGZM

A=B, B=C, C=D, D=E, E=F, F=G, G=H, H=I, I=J,
J=K, K=L, L=M, M=N, N=O, O=P, P=Q, Q=R, R=S,
S=T, T=U, U=V, V=W, W=X, X=Y, Y=Z, Z=A

8. REMEMBERED FOREVER

Julius Caesar was a great Roman leader. He was a brave man who had many friends. But he had many enemies too. They got together and killed him on March 15, 44 BC. Many people remember Julius Caesar on this day. They call it the 'Ides of March'. But did you know that we have days and dates because of Julius Caesar? And that he helped make our calendar? In fact, there's a month in the calendar named after him. Cross out the letters that appear thrice and put the rest together to form this month's name.

FBNAABMJUMN BE LMEYAENFF

9. A NOBLE MAN

Here's a picture of a very famous man. Some of the world's most important prizes are named after him. But oops! Whoever wrote the note forgot to write some letters. You can see these letters scattered on the page. Put them in the correct places.

OBAMA

ALFRED NOBEL

d c r m q t e

Alfred Nobel was a scientist from Swede_. He was born on the 21st of Octo_er 1833. He was a very clever man. He invented the d_namite and over three _undred other things! Isn't that quite an ac_ievement?

Mr Nobel never did get married. He didn't have any children. He was very rich. But he was also very _ise. He decided to leave his _oney to some very special people. They would be the ones who would make the world a better place. They would be people like d_ctors, scientists, wr_ters, economists and peacemakers. They would be from the fields of medicine, _hemistry, physics, literat_re and _conomics. Some of them would also be those working for world peace. And the rewar_s given to them would be called the Nobel Pri_es.

Mr Nobel died on the 10th of December in 1896. Five years later, Wilhelm Roentgen was awarded the very first Nobel Prize. He was a Germ_n scientist who had disco_ered _-rays.

Since then, the winners of the Nobel Prizes gather in Sweden's capital Stoc_holm every Decembe_. They meet Sweden's King and Queen at a ceremony where they all get _old medals and di_lomas. They also receive some of Mr Nobel's money. Everyone then attends a grand ban_uet.

You might know some of the Nobel Prize winners. They are also called Nobel _aureates. President Barack Obama of the United State_ of America is one of them. So was India's Mother Teresa. _ust like Mr Obama, she too wanted to make the world a more peace_ul place.

Scientists Thomas Edison, Albert Eins_ein and Marie Curie won Nobel Prizes too. You can read more about them in this book!

f b p o w u n k j h g a i l x y z v

10. THE MEN IN THEIR BOATS

These men from Scandinavian countries of Denmark, Sweden and Norway were famous for their long and narrow dragon-headed boats. They would row to the seaside villages of Northern Europe. While some of them wanted to loot villagers, the others only wanted new homes. What were these men called? The seven letters in their name are hidden in the picture. Find them and write them in the blank spaces below.

11. LADY WITH THE LAMP

Can you help Florence Nightingale find her way to the hospital? She was a young nurse from England in the 1800s. She nursed several British soldiers who were wounded in war. Florence also made the hospitals cleaner and showed the world how important nurses are.

12. DA VINCI'S HOMELAND

Leonardo da Vinci lived during the 15th century. Many people think he was one of the most talented men to have walked on Earth. But do you know which country Leonardo da Vinci came from? Read the notes and look out for the highlighted letters. Then put these letters in the blank spaces to find out the country's name.

Leonardo Da Vinci came from _ _ _ _

1. Leonardo da Vinci painted the Mona Lisa. It is the world's most famous painting.

2. Leonardo da Vinci loved birds. He often bought caged ones, just to set them free.

3. Leonardo da Vinci wanted to invent the helicopter, centuries before it was actually invented.

4. Leonardo da Vinci would often write backwards. That would make peeking into his diary quite difficult!

13. THE BROTHERS AND THEIR WHEELS

Everyone knows Orville and Wilbur Wright, the two American brothers who invented the airplane. But do you know where the Wright Brothers got many of their airplane-building ideas? It was in a shop they owned. The brothers sold another very famous mode of transport from this shop. Break the code to find out what it was.

__ __ __ __ __ __ __

1A 2E 3D 4A 5B 6C 7E

	1	2	3	4	5	6	7
A	B	U	Q	Y	N	Q	U
B	J	X	T	J	C	J	N
C	Q	O	X	O	P	L	W
D	A	J	C	Q	H	F	K
E	N	I	Q	N	O	N	E

14. ALL THE WORLD'S A STAGE

William Shakespeare was born many centuries ago but his plays are famous even today. This great playwright built The Globe, a theatre in London to stage his plays. Women weren't allowed to act so men played their parts. But there was a famous woman who came to watch Shakespeare's plays. The letters that form her name are scrambled below. Follow the arrows to unscramble them.

EUQEN BZALEEITH EHT STIFR

_ _ _ _ _   _ _ _ _ _ _ _ _ _ _   _ _ _   _ _ _ _ _

15. ON THE SILK ROAD

It's 1271. 17-year-old Marco Polo has just left his home in Venice, Italy and is headed to China. Once Marco gets there, he will become the Chinese Emperor Kublai Khan's trusted friend. Marco will also join the Emperor's court and visit many other Asian countries. But first, Marco must get to China safely. Help Marco make his way via the Silk Road and get to China.

YOU WILL NEED

- Two small coins
- Dice
- A friend (If no one is around, take turns and play with the second coin yourself!)

HOW TO PLAY

1. Roll your dice.
2. Move your coin forward by the number of spaces showed by the dice.
3. Follow the instructions on the tiles, if you land on it.
4. The player whose coin reaches China first is the winner.

3
4
5
6
7
8
9
10
11
12
13
14
19
20
21
Slow down to climb the high Pamir Mountains. Go back one space.
22
23
24
25
26
27
28
Join a caravan. Move two spaces ahead.
36
37
38
39
40
41
Bad health. Go back one space.
42
43
44
el refreshed at an oasis.
forward two spaces.

16. UP AND AWAY!

The Montgolfier Brothers sent a sheep, a duck and a rooster up to the sky—in the enormous hot air balloon they had invented. Marie Antoinette, the Queen of France, and her husband King Louis the XVI were watching the world's first hot air balloon passengers too! Find out which year it was by solving the number problems.

A. $1 \div 1 = ?$

B. $49 \div 7 = ?$

C. $20 - 12 = ?$

D. $83 + 54 - 134 = ?$

A.	B.	C.	D.

17. RING! RING!

On February 14, 1876, Alexander Graham Bell and Elisha Gray rushed to the patents office in the United States of America. Both of them wanted to tell the world that they had invented the telephone. But who got there first and who missed being known as the telephone's inventor just because he reached a little later? Add up the numbers shown on the paths. The inventor whose path has the lower total reached first and came to be known as the telephone's inventor.

18. A NOVEL IDEA

Charles Dickens lived in the 1800s. He worked at a shoe polish factory when he was a boy. But he went on to become one of the world's most famous writers. His homeland, England, was so proud of him that they even put his picture on a currency note. You can see Dickens at work here, with some of his most famous novels on the desk. Read their names and find them in the grid.

D	A	V	I	D	C	O	P	P	E	R	F	I	E	L	D	L
M	C	B	L	U	E	S	U	B	R	O	B	I	N	C	R	O
O	H	X	Q	R	H	Z	J	L	A	S	B	I	D	O	P	V
G	R	E	A	T	E	X	P	E	C	T	A	T	I	O	N	S
B	I	J	B	Y	M	Y	H	A	R	D	T	I	M	E	S	I
Y	S	I	J	Z	V	A	W	K	V	U	T	P	B	A	N	N
I	T	P	O	T	T	R	E	H	R	Y	R	A	J	O	P	T
D	M	W	T	A	S	Y	T	O	V	S	Q	O	Y	S	L	R
K	A	N	Q	B	J	B	L	U	B	R	B	G	A	B	O	H
A	S	P	A	A	S	S	G	S	T	O	I	N	D	I	L	O
I	C	V	A	N	H	O	I	E	B	A	J	O	O	J	A	T
H	A	B	U	I	M	H	E	C	O	R	S	T	M	Y	Q	M
K	R	Z	E	A	T	D	N	I	B	A	B	S	H	C	L	I
O	O	L	I	V	E	R	T	W	I	S	T	J	L	J	K	E
M	L	Q	L	I	T	T	L	E	D	O	R	R	I	T	R	S

A CHRISTMAS CAROL
DAVID COPPERFIELD
OLIVER TWIST
BLEAK HOUSE
LITTLE DORRIT
GREAT EXPECTATIONS
HARD TIMES

19. THE PHARAOH WHO BUILT PYRAMIDS

The Great Pyramid of Egypt is one of the oldest wonders of the world. It was also the world's tallest building for over four thousand years. But do you know who built the Great Pyramid? It was an ancient Egyptian pharaoh. Read the clues to find the pharaoh's name.

20. THE GREAT ENTERTAINER

When he was little, he got into trouble for taking his pet mouse to school. But when he grew up, everyone loved Mickey, his cartoon mouse. He made many famous movies and even built an enormous amusement park. But very few people know that he drove an ambulance during the First World War. Read out the picture clue to get this famous American's name.

+ t

-h+

21. FANTASTIC FRANKLIN

Most people fly kites for fun. But American scientist Benjamin Franklin used his kite to discover that lightning was actually very useful. Put together the 11 letters scattered around this picture to find out what he discovered in lightning.

____

22. THE LITTLE TRAMP

Some people can make you laugh with their jokes. But very few can make you laugh without saying a word. Charlie Chaplin could do just that. This English actor and filmmaker, born in late 1800, was famous for his funny tricks, small moustache and oversized pants. Spot five differences between the two pictures of Sir Charlie.

23. A GREAT LOVER OF NATURE

This Englishman went sailing to faraway places in the Beagle, his ship. He rode on giant tortoises and was often chased by angry ostriches. He learnt more about nature and was the first person to talk about how living things changed with time. Follow the arrows from the letters and fill in the blanks to find out what his name was.

24. THE BOY KING

Many people call him King Tut for short. But he was just a little boy when he took over Egypt's throne thousands of years ago. He died when he was just eighteen. But his mummified body is among the world's greatest treasures. Find out what this young king's name was. It's written here using symbols. They are just like the ones the ancient Egyptians used. Look at the symbols below to know what letters they stand for.

25. TELLER OF TALES

Fables are stories about animals that teach us life lessons. One of the most famous writers of fables was a man from Greece. He lived thousands of years ago. But children love his fables with foxes, crows, hares, tortoises and birds even today. Drop one letter from the name of the object to get the answer to the word clue. Join the dropped letters to find out the name of this famous writer of fables.

You wear this on your head.

- - -

It helps people travel to different places.

- - - - -

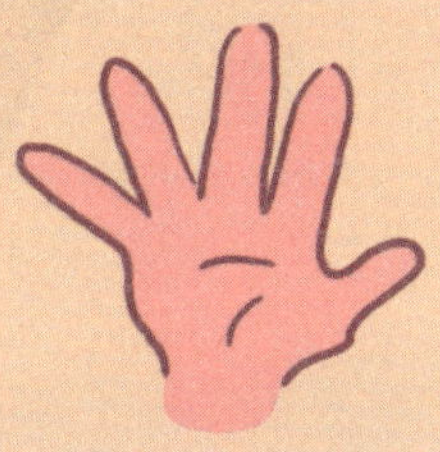

You find this on a beach.

- - - -

You eat ice-cream in this.

- - - -

A juicy fruit.

- - - -

The name of this Greek fable writer was _ _ _ _ _.

26. MEET THE MASTER

This talented artist and sculptor lived in Italy in the 1400s. He designed many famous buildings too. Find out what the name of this great master was by solving the puzzle. We've started it by circling "M". Now circle every alternate letter. The circled letters will lead you to this master's name.

M _ _ _ _ _ _ _ _ _ _ _

27. SCIENCE'S SUPERHERO

Albert Einstein's teachers didn't want him in their school because they thought he wasn't very bright. But Einstein grew up to become the world's greatest scientist. And when he died, his brain was stored for other scientists to study. Though Albert Einstein chose to live in the United States of America, he was born in another country. Solve the picture clue to find out the name of this country.

_ _ _ _ _ _ _

28. EUREKA!

Sir Isaac Newton was a brilliant man. He created the colour wheel. He showed the world how sunlight is made of many colours, just like the rainbow. One day, a fruit fell on Sir Netwon's head. It helped him discover gravity—the invisible force that keeps everything in place. Find out which fruit it was by filling up the blank spaces with the letters that have the colours of Sir Newton's colour wheel.

29. THE BOY WHO WANTED TO READ

This lad from France lost his eyesight when he was just three. But by the time he turned 15, he found a way to read. The set of letters he created, by arranging raised dots, gave a chance to sightless people to read. Find out his name by breaking the code.

30. AROUND THE WORLD

In 1520, Ferdinand Magellan, a Portuguese explorer, became the first person to go all around the world. He found his way to the Pacific Ocean, which he called "Mar Pacífico", or "Peaceful Sea". Help him find his way through the maze.

31. NAPOLEON'S HAT

Napoleon Bonaparte wore many different hats. He was the first emperor of France. He was a great military leader too. But there was another hat that Napoleon was very famous for. You can see him wearing it here. Napoleon wore this hat so stylishly that it became his symbol. Which one of the hats shown below do you think is identical to the one Napoleon wore?

32. A MAN OF PEACE

His parents named him Mohandas Karamchand Gandhi. Many people called him the Little Brown Saint. But when he used peace to make the British leave India, he became one of the world's greatest leaders. He was also honoured with a new title meaning "great soul". Find out what this title was. Fill the boxes with the names of these two very famous monuments. Then put the letters from the shaded boxes together to find out Gandhi's title.

T		J	■	M				L

Q	U			B	■		I	N		R

M						

33. BURNING BRIGHT

American scientist Thomas Edison made the light bulb glow brighter and longer. He also made it more affordable. Solve the maths problems below to find out which year Mr. Edison achieved this in.

A. $1 \div 1 = ?$

B. $3 \times 3 - 1 = ?$

C. $12 - 5 = ?$

D. $16 \div 3 = ?$

A.	B.	C.	D.

34. THE X-FACTOR

Marie Curie was the first and only woman to win two Nobel Prizes. She discovered radium, a metal no one knew of. She also helped many soldiers wounded during the First World War by inventing a mobile X-ray machine. Though Madame Curie lived in France, she was born in another country. To find out the name of this country cross out all the letters that appear thrice. The rest of the letters will form the country's name.

ECBHHPCOLBCANHEDBE

_ _ _ _ _ _

35. THE MESSENGER

Long, long ago, lived a man named Pheidippides. He went all over Greece carrying messages. One day, Pheidippides had to carry a message to Athens from a battleground. He ran as fast as he could, without even stopping to rest. The Athenians rejoiced at Pheidippides's message. It was good news for them. But sadly, it was Pheidippides's last message. Pheidippides had grown so tired that he fell asleep forever. In his memory, a popular race was named after the battleground Pheidippides last ran from. Write the first two letters of all the objects shown to form this race and battlefield's name.

 +  +  + 

___ ___ ___ ___ ___ ___ ___ ___

= ___ ___ ___ ___ ___ ___ ___ ___

36. IDEA IN A BATHTUB

Archimedes was a scientist and inventor who lived in ancient Greece. One day, the king summoned him. The king was worried that his goldsmith had replaced some gold with silver while making his crown, even though the crown looked like it was made of solid gold. No one could solve the mystery. But Archimedes soaked the crown in his bathtub and solved it. At the same time, he also discovered a very important law of physics. And oops! He ran to tell the king about it, forgetting to wear his clothes! Here are some pictures of what happened that day. But they are not in order. Number the pictures in the correct order.

37. THE WICKED HORSEMEN

The Great Wall of China is the longest wall in the world. But did you know that the Chinese Emperor Qin built it to keep away fierce horsemen who would invade ancient China from the north and turn everything topsy-turvy? Oops! The letters in their name have turned topsy-turvy too. Can you turn them around?

38. THE INCREDIBLE MAGICIAN

He was born Ehrich Weiss in Hungary but grew up in the United States of America. He could do incredible things, like walking through walls, making elephants disappear and escaping from locked boxes while his hands were tied. Find out what the most famous magician in the world was better known as. Fill the boxes with name of things magicians use while performing tricks. Put the letters of the shaded boxes together to get this magician's stage name.

_ _ T

L _ _ K

H _ N _ C _ _ _ S

C _ _ _ S

C _ _ N S

W _ _ D

R _ B _ _ T

_ _ _ _ _ _ _

39. THE DOG WHO WENT TO SPACE

Long ago, in 1957, a real dog was sent around the Earth's orbit by her country Russia. The letters in her name appear here on the stars whose value equals 21. Put these letters together in the blank spaces below to get the name of the first dog in space.

L 7 X 3

A 25-4

R 8 X 4

I 21/1

B 19+3

K 42/2

A 5 + 6 + 10

40. A GREAT EMPRESS

Catherine the Great was a Russian empress. She made Russia one of the world's biggest countries during her reign in the 1700s and ruled for almost 30 long years. Catherine is a long name too. How many three-letter words can you make from it?

41. NOT WITHOUT HIS HORSE

No one could defeat Alexander the Great. He was a fearless prince and commander who lived in Macedonia over two thousand years ago. Alexander had conquered almost the whole world on his favourite horse. He was so fond of his horse that he even named an ancient city after it. Solve the puzzle below to find out the horse's name. We've started the puzzle by circling the letter "B". All you have to do is circle every alternate letter to find the horse's name.

B _ _ _ _ _ _ _ _ _ _ _

42. THE LIBERATOR

Simón Bolívar lived in the 19th century. He was South America's greatest hero who helped free six countries from the Spanish rule. The names of these countries have been written on the signboard below. But oops! The hungry llama has bitten off some of their letters. Can you complete the names of the countries?

43. MAKING MUSIC IN SILENCE

You wouldn't be able to listen to music if you didn't have ears. But imagine making beautiful music when you can no longer hear. Well, that's exactly what this famous 18th century musician from Germany could do. Find out what his name was by solving the puzzle.

Lud + 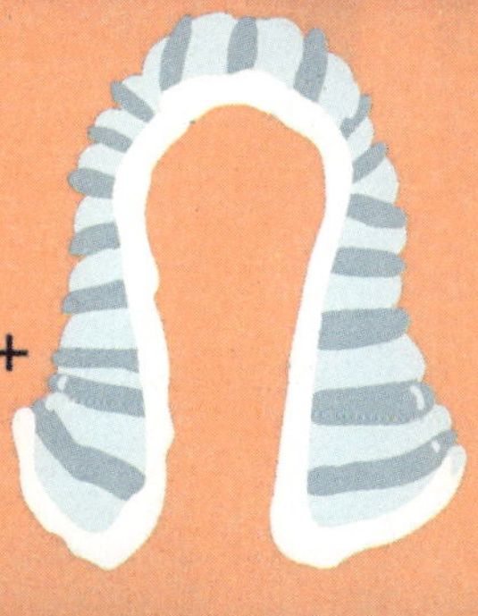 van Beeth 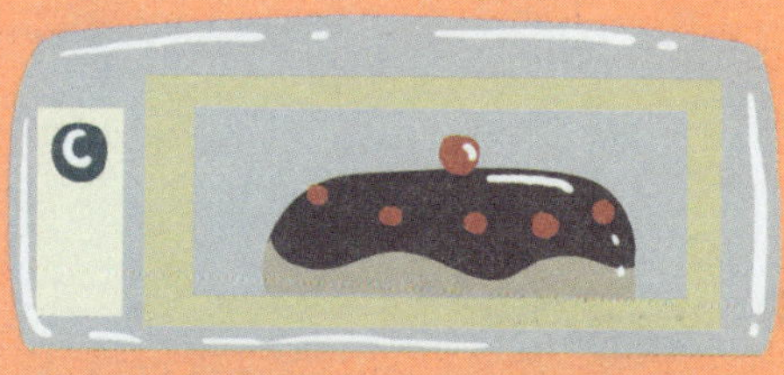

44. RACE TO THE BOTTOM OF THE WORLD

In 1911, Roald Amundsen from Norway and Robert Scott from the United Kingdom of Great Britain raced to get to the South Pole on the icy and windy continent of Antarctica. But which one of them reached first? Add up the numbers shown on each path. The one whose path has the lower total was the one who reached the South Pole first.

45. SCALING THE WORLD'S HIGHEST MOUNTAIN

The whole world thought that Mount Everest, the world's highest mountain, was impossible to climb. But in 1953, Edmund Hillary from New Zealand and Tenzing Norgay from Nepal proved everyone wrong. Draw a line connecting all the odd numbers. It will show you the route Hillary and Norgay took.

ANSWERS

1 **THE MILK MAN**
Louis Pasteur

2 **THE GENIUS FROM PISA**
The objects are a tent and a pear.
Galileo helped make the telescope.

3 **THE EXPLORER'S SHIPS**
Santa Maria
Nina
Pinta

4 **WORLD'S FAVOURITE STORYTELLERS**
Grimm

5 **FIRST MEN ON THE MOON**
Neil Armstrong
Buzz Aldrin

6 **THE LITTLE MUSICIAN**
Wolfgang

7 **A LOVING HUSBAND**
Shah Jahan

8 **REMEMBERED FOREVER**
July

9 **A NOBEL MAN**
Alfred Nobel was a scientist from Sweden. He was born on the 21st of October 1833. He was a very clever man. He invented the dynamite and over three hundred other things! Isn't that quite an achievement?

Mr Nobel never did get married. He didn't have any children. He was very rich. But he was also very wise. He decided to leave his money to some very special people. They would be the ones who would make the world a better place. They would be people like doctors, scientists, writers, economists and peacemakers. They would be from the fields of medicine, chemistry, physics, literature and economics. Some of them would also be those working for world peace. And the rewards given to them would be called the Nobel Prizes.

Mr Nobel died on the 10th of December in 1896. Five years later, Wilhelm Roentgen was awarded the very first Nobel Prize. He was a German scientist who had discovered X-rays.

Since then, the winners of the Nobel Prizes gather in Sweden's capital Stockholm every December. They meet Sweden's king and queen at a ceremony where they all get gold medals and diplomas. They also receive some of Mr Nobel's money. Everyone then attends a grand banquet.

You might know some of the Nobel Prize winners. They are also called Nobel laureates. President Barack Obama of the United States of America is one of them. So was India's Mother Teresa. Just like Mr Obama, she too wanted to make the world a more peaceful place.

Scientists Thomas Edison, Albert Einstein and Marie Curie won Nobel Prizes too. You can read more about them in this book!

10 THE MEN IN THEIR BOATS

11 THE LADY WITH THE LAMP

12 DA VINCI'S HOMELAND

Leonardo Da Vinci came from ITALY.

13 THE BROTHERS AND THEIR WHEELS

Bicycle

14 ALL THE WORLD'S A STAGE

Queen Elizabeth The First

16 UP AND AWAY!

1783

17 RING! RING!

Alexander Graham Bell's pathway: 40.
Elisha Gray's pathway: 45.
Since Bell reached the Patents Office before Gray that day, he was known as the inventor of the telephone.

18 A NOVEL IDEA

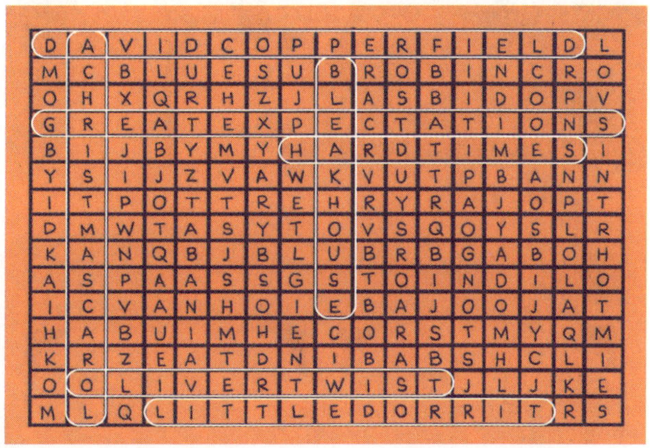

19 THE PHARAOH WHO BUILT PYRAMIDS

Pharaoh Khufu.

20 THE GREAT ENTERTAINER

Walt Disney

21 FANTASTIC FRANKLIN

Electricity

22 THE LITTLE TRAMP

23 A GREAT LOVER OF NATURE

Charles Darwin

24 THE BOY KING

Tutankhamun

25 TELLER OF TALES

C **A** P
P L A N **E**
S A N D
C **O** N E
P E A R

The name of the Greek fable writer was AESOP.

26 MEET THE MASTER

Michelangelo

27 SCIENCE'S SUPERHERO

Germany

28 EUREKA!

Apple

29 THE BOY WHO WANTED TO READ

Louis Braille

30 AROUND THE WORLD

31 **NAPOLEON'S HAT**
Hat C is identical to Napoleon's hat.

32 **A MAN OF PEACE**

T A J ■ M A H A L

Q U T U B ■ M I N A R

Mohandas Gandhi was called

M A H A T M A

33 **BURNING BRIGHT**
1879

34 **THE X-FACTOR**
Poland

35 **THE MESSENGER**
The objects are a mask, a ram, a thumb and an onion. Marathon is the name of the race and the battlefield Pheidippides ran from.

36 **IDEA IN A BATH TUB**

37 **WICKED HORSEMEN**
Huns

38 **THE INCREDIBLE MAGICIAN**

H A T
L O C K
H A N D C U F F S
C A R D S
C O I N S
W A N D
R A B B I T
H O U D I N I

39 **THE DOG WHO WENT TO SPACE**
L
7 x 3=21

A
5 + 6 + 10=21

I
21/1=21

K
42/2=21

A
25-4=21
Laika

40 **A GREAT EMPRESS**
ace, act, air, ant, arc, are, art, ate, can, car, cat, ear, eat, era, ere, hat, hen, her, hit, ice, ire, net, nit, ran, rat, tan, tar, tea, ten, the, tie, tin. We got 32 words in all. How many did you get?

41 **NOT WITHOUT HIS HORSE**
Bucephalus

42 **THE LIBERATOR**

Colombia
Panama
Bolivia
Ecuador
Peru
Venezuela

43 **MAKING MUSIC IN SILENCE**

Ludwig van Beethoven

44 **RACE TO THE BOTTOM OF THE WORLD**

The numbers on Roald Amundsen's pathway add up to 18. Those on Robert Scott's add up to 20. Amundsen reached the South Pole first. Scott reached five days later.

45 **SCALING THE WORLD'S HIGHEST MOUNTAIN**

Pooja Lulla is the author of more than 35 books for children. They include picture books, graphic novels, chapter books and encyclopedias. She has also written the very popular *Around the World in 80 Puzzles*, *Animal Puzzles* and *The Big Book of Festival Puzzles* (also published by Scholastic). Pooja also writes lyrics for children's songs, scripts for cartoon shows and designs computer games. She lives in Mumbai.

Shreya Sen is a children's book illustrator based out of Kolkata. Her earliest memories are of her mom dragging her to book fairs in Assam. Her favourite pastime was to gorge on Russian picture books and draw on the walls. This led to her studying Animation Film Design at NID, Ahmedabad. A summer internship at a children's publication house made her believe that this is what she wants to do for the rest of her life.

OTHER BOOKS BY THE AUTHOR

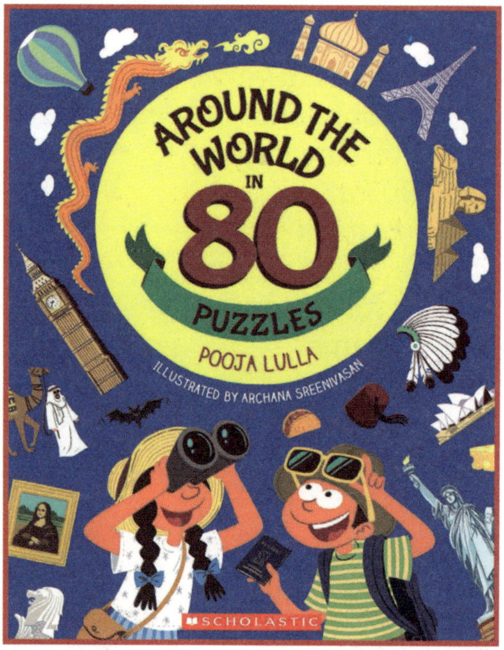

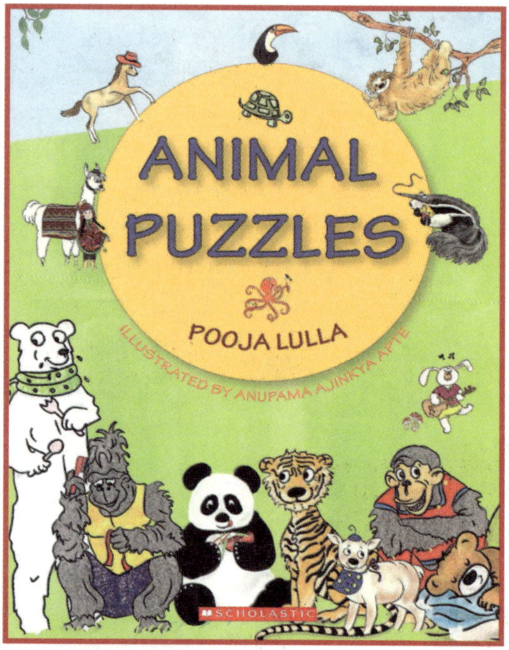